Text copyright © 1991 by Gloria Whelan.
Illustrations copyright © 1991 by Leslie Bowman.
Cover art copyright © 1993 by Leslie Bowman.
All rights reserved. Published by Scholastic Inc., 555 Broadway, New York, NY 10012, by arrangement with Alfred A. Knopf, Inc.
Printed in the U.S.A.
ISBN 0-590-62361-3

8 9 10   40   02 01

Hannah

By Gloria Whelan

Illustrated by Leslie Bowman

SCHOLASTIC INC.

New York   Toronto   London   Auckland   Sydney

1

It was the fall of 1887. I heard Papa's horse and wagon before my brother, Johnny, and sister, Verna, did. Because I can't see, I listen harder than they do. Ever since I learned the new teacher was coming to board with us, I tried to imagine what she would look like. I thought she might be heaped into a round, soft shape like the big pile of laundry Mama does on Mondays, or she might be tall and straight and hard like the oak tree that grows next to the porch. I wondered what her voice would be like and hoped it would have the gentle sound of a mourning dove on a summer day.

When the buggy pulled up, everyone rushed to the window to see her. I just stayed put. I had been told often enough to keep out of the way so I wouldn't get knocked over when people were rushing around. Verna didn't forget me, though. She called out, "Hannah, the teacher's pretty! She's got a big puff of brown hair and a lace collar on her jacket."

"Never mind pretty," Mama said. "Pretty doesn't make a good teacher."

We were picked to have the teacher live with us because our farm was the nearest one to the school after the Bonners' farm. The Bonners couldn't board teachers any more because they were getting too old. Even though it would mean more work for her, Mama looked forward to having the teacher. Our nearest neighbor was Mr. Peterson, and there were no women on his farm, so the teacher would be company for Mama. Papa liked the idea of having the teacher too, because she would pay us a dollar a week for her room and three meals a day. It was money you could count on, not like money you got from the winter wheat, that might freeze, or the corn, that could dry up if the rain didn't come.

"Here's the new teacher, Miss Lydia Robbin," said Papa.

Lydia, I thought. What a beautiful name. I said it over to myself. It was like the sound of Mama's silk dress sliding off when she got home from church.

Papa was introducing us. "This here is Martha, my wife. And Verna, she's eleven. Johnny, he's six. And Hannah, she's nine."

Miss Robbin said "How do you do" to each one of us. When she came to me, Mama said, "You needn't shake hands with Hannah. She can't see you, nor anything else, poor thing."

Everyone around us had always known I was blind, so it was only when a stranger came that it had to be explained. Even though I had grown used to it, I didn't like to hear it said out loud. But Mama claimed it was a "fact of life" that had to be faced.

I felt someone take hold of my hand and squeeze it gently. I knew it must be Miss Robbin's hand, because it was soft and smooth. One of Papa's hands had a finger missing where he got it caught in the combine. Mama's hands were rough from all the washing up and digging in the vegetable garden. Johnny's hands were little and sort of damp because he still sucked his thumb. Verna's hands felt raggedy at the nails because she bit them. "How do you do, Hannah," Miss Robbin said. "I look forward to having your three children in my class, Mrs. Thomas."

Mama said, "Verna and Johnny won't give you any trouble. Hannah doesn't go to

school. There's no point to it." Mama's plain-spoken, but I guess what she said sounded a little hard even to her. She knows how I hate it when Verna and Johnny leave me behind in the morning. So she added, "Hannah keeps me company."

"Well, we must see about that," Miss Robbin said. Her voice wasn't as soft and polite as it was at first.

"There's nothing to see about," Papa said. "No point in buying books and clothes for someone who can't see to learn. Now, I expect you'd like Martha to show you where your room is. I'll get your trunk from the wagon."

As soon as we were alone, I said to Verna and Johnny, "Tell me what she looks like."

Verna said, "She's a little thing, but she stands up straight. Her eyes are blue. Her complexion is all white and pink. Her jacket has little buttons down the front and a sort of ruffle in the back."

Miss Robbin sounded elegant. I sighed and wondered what I looked like to her. I hoped she wouldn't notice that my hand-me-down dress from Verna was too large for me. I knew my hair was tangled too. When it was long, like now, I had trouble combing it. Mama had been so busy she had forgotten to cut it.

"Even though she's little, I think she'll be able to handle the older boys," said Verna. Last year's teacher whined all the time about how bad the older boys were. They threw erasers across the schoolroom and didn't do their lessons. They even tipped the privy over one night. The teacher complained, but she never did anything.

Verna and Johnny were good about telling me what happened at school, but it wasn't the same as being there. I would have given just about anything to go to school.

2

The next day was Sunday. It was my favorite day because I got to go to church. The church was five miles away, so we all crowded into the wagon.

"Where were you before you came to us?" Mama asked Miss Robbin. Mama likes to know all there is to know about someone.

"I was born downstate, in Flint. When I was only a baby, my mother and father died of typhoid, and I went to live with my aunt and uncle on their farm. My uncle died six years ago. I lost my aunt last winter. I was teaching in a school near their farm, but after my aunt died, I decided to make a new start someplace else. I could never live in a city,

so when I heard about the school up here in northern Michigan and how you had lakes nearby and woods, it seemed a perfect place."

"Well, I don't know that you'll have much time to go walking in the woods or along the lakes, but it *is* pretty country," said Mama. "My husband's father homesteaded here. We've made a living off the farm, but not much more. You won't find things fancy." Then, because Mama was softer-hearted than she let on, she said, "I hope you don't feel too bad about your aunt's passing."

I felt her stretch her arm out, and I guessed she had taken hold of Miss Robbin's hand, because the teacher said, "I just thank the Lord that I have come to a kind family. If I do or say anything you don't think right, you must let me know."

But this show of feeling was too much for Mama. She took her hand back and made some remark about how warm it was for

October. Our schools always started the first week in October and went until January. In the winter there was so much snow on the roads, school closed down. The snow got so high, even the sleighs couldn't manage. Papa often had to dig a tunnel through the snow to the chicken house and the barn. In April school opened again. It went on until August. After that children helped to harvest the corn and wheat.

In church I waited for the choir to come down the aisle singing, "Holy, holy, holy." That always half-thrilled and half-scared me. Since I couldn't see anything, I was never sure but what God wasn't right in the church looking at me. Pastor Olsen's sermons were long, and my back got tired from sitting up straight. Sometimes Pastor Olsen would read a Psalm from the Bible. I would try to say the words over in my head so that I could keep some of them. Especially the Psalm where the mountains skip like rams and the little hills like lambs. Or the one where the precious ointment runs all the way down Aaron's beard to the hem of his garment.

After church everyone clustered around us to meet the new teacher. People don't often come to settle around here, so a new face causes a stir. After they were introduced to Miss Robbin, they said a few words of greeting to Mama and Papa and asked me, "And how is poor Hannah today?" I was always "poor Hannah," like it was one word.

When we were back in the wagon, Miss Robbin asked me, "Why do they call you 'poor Hannah'?"

"Because I can't see," I said.

"If it comes to that," Miss Robbin told me, "all of us have things we don't see. I would guess, Hannah, that you see some things people with perfectly good eyes don't."

"We've never pretended to Hannah that she was like other children," Mama said. "We believe in facing up to facts."

"Oh, but surely, Mrs. Thomas, Hannah is like other children."

"No, she's not. I don't say there's anything bad about her, mind you. She's good company for me when the other children are away at school and Mr. Thomas is out in the fields. I couldn't ask for better. She can make up a story right out of her head that you wouldn't believe."

"I suppose you would miss her if she went to school?" Miss Robbin asked. For a moment I got so excited by the thought of being able to go to school, my breath stopped.

"Well, she's not going to go," Mama said. And for the first time I wondered if Mama was keeping me home from school because I wouldn't do well there or because she just wanted me for herself.

I got to sit next to Miss Robbin at Sunday dinner. She smelled of something nice. It wasn't strong like the perfume Mama kept in a little bottle on her dresser and never used. It was more like fresh lemonade. Mama went to a lot of trouble to make a good dinner for Miss Robbin. "I don't want the teacher telling other families she doesn't get a decent meal here," Mama said. We had all my favorite things: roast chicken and mashed potatoes with lots of gravy, and biscuits. For dessert there was apple pie sweetened with maple sugar from our own sugarbush. Mama cut my meat for me. When I heard the milk jug being passed around, I held my mug out so Mama could pour for me.

"I'll show you how to pour your own milk, Hannah," Miss Robbin said.

"She'll only make a mess of it," said Mama.

But Miss Robbin told me to put my finger inside my mug. "Here is the pitcher, Hannah. Just pour very slowly until you feel the milk with your finger. Then stop right away."

Everyone was quiet. I knew they were watching me, and I worried about spilling

the milk. It wasn't so much that I was afraid of making Mama angry with me but that I didn't want her to be angry with Miss Robbin. I poured as carefully as I could, and as soon as I felt the cold milk on my finger, I stopped and held out the pitcher for someone to take.

"Very good," said Miss Robbin. Her words sounded a little strange. In our house no one praised you for doing something right. It was just expected of you. Miss Robbin had nice things to say about Mama's cooking too. "Mrs. Thomas, this chicken is so tender, I can cut it with my fork. And I've never tasted lighter biscuits. If I didn't keep my hand on them, I think they would float right up to the ceiling."

Johnny giggled. I could tell by the way Mama insisted that the chicken was stringy and the potatoes lumpy and the biscuits too well done—none of which was true—that she was pleased. The more you said nice things to Mama, the more she fought them off.

After lunch Miss Robbin said, "I ate so much, I can hardly take a breath. I'll have to walk some of that delicious dinner off. Hannah, will you come with me?"

I jumped up eagerly. It wasn't often that someone asked me to walk with them. They usually got tired of holding my hand and telling me to look out for things.

"I don't know that it's healthy to take a walk after a big meal," Mama said. I began to feel Mama and Miss Robbin were each pulling at me from different sides. I wasn't sure I liked being in the middle.

"Nonsense," Papa said. "I go out and plow a field after a big dinner six days a week." I could have hugged him.

3

I knew the sun was shining, because I could feel its warmth like a wool shawl all along my arms and shoulders. There were no leaves under my feet, so I guessed they were still on the oak trees. Soon they would fall. Already I could hear the acorns dropping on our roof. "Why don't you show me around the farm, Hannah," Miss Robbin said.

"I wouldn't know how to," I told her. "Nobody ever showed me." I could get from the house to the privy, and sometimes Verna and I would go for a walk, but I didn't know where anything was or even what was there. I knew we had horses and cows and pigs, because Papa talked about them and I could hear them, but I didn't know where they were or exactly what they were like.

"Well, in that case, Hannah," Miss Robbin said, "I guess I'll have to show *you*. We'll start with the barn. Run your hand along the fence and count your steps, and you'll know how to get there yourself next time. This is the barn. Don't step off the walk or you'll get your feet dirty. Here's the first cow. Just feel her, Hannah. Feel how smooth and warm she is. Now run your hand over her face. Feel how long her eyelashes are, and now feel under her belly. This is where the milk comes from. I'm sure your father could teach you how to milk a cow."

We went to the stable and I felt our horses, Billy and Maggie. Then we went to the pen where the pigs were. It didn't smell very good there, but I got to feel some little piglets

and even held one in my arms until it wriggled away. We went into the chicken coop, and I felt a rush of air as the chickens flew out of our way. Miss Robbin put my hand on the warm, smooth eggs in the nests. The eggs were traded for sugar and salt at the general store. The farm grew larger and larger in my mind. I felt almost dizzy. "What else is there?" I kept asking. "What else is there?"

Finally Miss Robbin said, "I think you're getting too excited, Hannah. We'll save the rest for another day. Let's just walk out to your father's woods and find a nice cool spot." As we went, Miss Robbin told me what she saw. "The wild asters are blooming, Hannah. Here, feel what they are like. Smell them."

The flowers were small in my hand. Each one had tiny petals and a center like a little covered button. Their smell was dry and sharp. "The milkweed pods are open," Miss

Robbin said. She put something in my hand that was as soft as anything I had ever felt. "There are thousands of soft things like that," she said, "each one with a seed. They'll float in the air, and wherever they come down there will be more milkweed plants. Here is a nice mossy place where we can sit." I settled down beside her, feeling spongy, thick moss under my hand. "Your mother tells me you make up stories, Hannah. Would you tell me one?"

Suddenly, I was shy. It was one thing to tell my mama a story while she was dusting or kneading bread and only half-listening. It was something else to tell Miss Robbin. She would hear every word I said and might think my story foolish. Still, she had been so nice to me, I couldn't bring myself to say no.

"Once there was a horse named Billy, just like our horse," I began. "By day he pulled a plow, but at night whenever the moon shone on him he became Nebuchadnezzar.

You could fly through the sky on him. You could go anywhere in the world and see anything you wanted to see. You could fly over Jerusalem and Solomon's Temple, covered with gold and garnished with precious stones. You could see Queen Victoria drinking tea in Buckingham Palace. You could see whales swimming in the ocean. On the way home you could fly over old Mr. Peterson's house and see his dog that gets around on three legs. . . ."

"You know, Hannah," said Miss Robbin, "books are like your horse, Nebuchadnezzar. When you read them, you can see wonderful things."

"But I'll never be able to read."

"Perhaps you will. First, we must ask your parents to let you go to school."

4

Monday came and Johnny and Verna went off to school. Miss Robbin had left early to get the schoolroom swept out and tidied for class. Verna knew I was sorry to be left behind. She promised she would tell me all about the first day of school.

When she got home, I was waiting for her. "Carl Kleino was throwing spitballs at the little kids," Verna said. "Miss Robbin said if he was going to act like a baby he would have to sit with the kindergarten and first grade. Carl's face was red as a beet. And you know what? Miss Robbin told the class that before long there might be a new pupil in school. I think she meant you."

After dinner that night while Miss Robbin was helping Mama with the dishes, she said real nicely, "I've only got twelve students, Mrs. Thomas. I'd have plenty of time to give Hannah some lessons if you'd let her come to school."

I held my breath and crossed my fingers.

"No point to it," Mama said.

Papa was sitting at the kitchen table. I smelled the kerosene lamp and heard his pencil scratch. I guessed he was adding up the bills and figuring out the ones he could pay. There had been almost no rain during the summer. Half of our crops had dried up. He said to Miss Robbin, "You won't get the missis to let Hannah go to school. She likes having a young one around the house. It looks as if Hannah's going to stay her baby no matter how old Hannah gets to be. You see a cow like that sometimes, won't let go of her calf."

Mama flew out at Papa, "Pa, that isn't so."

Miss Robbin said, "I'm sure Mrs. Thomas wouldn't stand in the way of giving Hannah an education."

"Well, you all seem to know more than I do," Mama said. "I guess Hannah can do what she wants to. But she's not going to like school when she finds out it'll be way over her head."

"And I can't pay for any books," Papa said.

The next morning I was the first one up. I climbed out of bed without waking Verna and put on my clothes. I crept down the stairs to the kitchen and pumped some water to wash my face and hands. To please Mama I set the table for breakfast. I made sure I had the forks on the left and the knives and spoons on the right. When Mama came down, she didn't say anything. But she didn't say I couldn't go to school. Miss Robbin didn't say anything either. I guess she thought now that she had her way it was best to keep quiet. She just thanked Mama for the breakfast and started off for school. As she went out the door she put her hand on my shoulder and gave it a squeeze.

When it was time for Verna and Johnny and me to go, I went over to hug Mama. She pushed me away and handed the three of us our jugs of water. There was no well at the school, so we had to bring our own water to drink and to wash our slates.

On the way to school Verna held my hand. I thought we would never get there. Finally I heard the voices of the other children. Miss Robbin came out to meet me. "Hannah," she said, "we're so happy to have you in school." But she didn't let me sit with Verna. She made me go up in front and sit with Johnny and the other little children. I remembered how Verna said it was a punishment when Carl had to sit there.

I listened to all the voices and tried to make out who they belonged to. There was an arithmetic lesson that didn't make any sense to me. Then there was some reading that I couldn't do. I began to wonder why I was there.

When it was time for recess, I started to walk out of school, feeling my way by holding on to the desks. As I got to the back of the room, I heard Carl say, "You sure can tell Hannah Thomas can't see in the mirror or she wouldn't look like a ragbag with a haystack for her hair." I was so mad I picked up a book from one of the desks and threw it in the direction of Carl's voice. I heard him cry out. Then someone stuck something out in front of my foot, and I tripped and fell on my face in the aisle.

Miss Robbin and Verna ran to help me up. "Carl Kleino," Miss Robbin said. Her

voice was sharp and cold like icicles. "I saw you trip Hannah. Go up in front of the room and stand by my desk. Your parents are going to hear about this. Hannah, are you hurt?" I shook my head. "You go out with the other children, and I'll come out in a minute. I want a word with Carl."

Verna led me outside. She tried to comfort me by telling me how Carl was always getting into trouble. "I don't think he likes being the oldest one in school," she said.

After a while one of Verna's girlfriends called to her to come and jump rope. "I'll just take one turn," Verna said, and ran off. I was just standing there by myself. I thought about how I hadn't been able to do any lessons and how no one talked to me. I wished I were with Mama. Suddenly, the only thing that seemed important was to get back home.

By going from tree to tree I felt my way down the path that led from the schoolyard to the road. Because I was moving through the trees, no one noticed me. When I reached the road, I was unsure about which way I should turn. I decided any way was better than staying at school. I had been there all morning and hadn't learned anything. Miss Robbin had hardly spoken to me.

Under my feet I felt the sandy road with its wagon ruts. At first I began to run along the road. Then I thought someone might see me, so I turned into the woods. There was no sun in the woods, and I hadn't taken my sweater. I began to shiver. Everything felt strange and unfriendly. Blackberry briars scratched my arms and snagged my hair. Branches slapped at me and tore my skirt. Every direction I turned seemed to lead me into more trouble. The ground gave way and slipped out from under me. I gave up, sinking down to my knees. At first I was too stubborn to call for help. Then, knowing I was lost, I cried out. There was no answer. I was sorry I had ever left my house, where my mother watched over me.

Once, Johnny had caught a field mouse and put it into a little box to keep it safe from owls and foxes. I thought at the time, even with the danger of owls and foxes, I would rather be free than live shut up in a box. Now I wanted to be shut up in the safe box of my house.

I sat there on the ground, hugging myself to keep warm. I could smell the pine trees and hear the scuffle and scratch of squirrels running along the ground. I thought of getting up and trying to find my way, but I was afraid I would lose myself deeper in the woods and no one would ever find me. It seemed like I had been sitting there shivering for hours when I heard Papa calling to me. I called back. At first he didn't hear me. "Papa," I called. "Here I am. Take me home. I want to go home."

Papa scooped me up and carried me to the wagon. "No need to cry, Hannah," he said. "You're all right now. We'll have you home in no time."

Mama was at the door to meet us. "She might have fallen into the lake," Mama said. "That's what comes of letting her do a foolish thing like going to school. Her place is right here with me."

5

Mama made me hot chocolate to drink and took me upstairs to my bed. I guess I fell asleep, because when I awoke I heard Miss Robbin's voice. "Hannah, I'm so sorry for what happened," she said. "I blame myself. I should have kept an eye on you, but I wanted you to be independent. I didn't want the children to think of you as the teacher's pet, but as a student just like themselves. I promise you, if you come back I'll see that you are never teased again."

"But you made me sit with the little children."

"That was just so I could be right there to help you when the time came for you to do your lessons. I had planned a special lesson for you after recess."

"Carl said mean things about the way I look."

"I'll help you change the way you look. I've got three yards of the prettiest muslin you can imagine in my trunk. It has little yellow daisies all over it. I'll cut out a dress for you and sew it this weekend. As for Carl, I don't think he means the things he says. He's unhappy because he wants to be outdoors working on his dad's farm instead of in school. He knows he isn't very good at schoolwork. I made a bargain with him. I told him that if he behaved and settled down to studying, I'd give him a whole week off during the potato harvest."

I didn't want to go back to school, but I had never had a dress all my own, just hand-me-downs from Verna. For a new dress, I thought I might go back to school. Just for a day.

Mama was against it. At supper that night when I said Miss Robbin would make me a new dress for school, Mama said, "Hannah, you've had all you are going to have of school."

Papa said, "Don't be hasty, Martha. What happened today set me to thinking. We can't let Hannah stay helpless. She has to learn to take care of herself. You and I aren't going to be around forever. The time will come when she's going to be on her own. She can't go getting lost every time she puts her foot out the door."

Nothing more was said, but when Saturday came, Miss Robbin began to make my new dress. Mama couldn't help herself exclaiming on how pretty the material was. "I don't see why you want to waste it on a little girl's dress," she said to Miss Robbin. "You've got more than enough there for a dress yourself."

"I'd rather see Hannah in the dress," Miss Robbin said. "Besides, it was my fault that Hannah tore her dress. I should have done a better job of watching over her."

I could tell from Mama's "humph" that she was getting a little more soft-hearted toward Miss Robbin.

"I'm putting a ruffle around the bottom of your skirt," Miss Robbin said to me. "Here, Hannah, you can feel it."

The material was soft when I touched it. It had a sharp new smell. Even the collar had a little ruffle around it.

Saturday evening, when we got the bathtub out and put it in the kitchen, Mama said, "Hannah, I believe I'll cut your hair before I wash it. It's looking kind of stringy." I guess

she didn't want Miss Robbin to be the only one to fuss over me. I could feel the weight of my hair grow lighter, and little pieces of it fell down my dress. "There now," Mama said when she had finished, "your hair crimps up into real pretty curls. It'll be easier for you to comb, too." And then, like she was choking down some bitter medicine, Mama added, ". . . when you have to get dressed for school."

I could hardly believe my ears. Mama was actually going to let me go back to school. I reached out and hugged her. "Heavens," Mama said, "there's no need for that." She began to pour the hot water from the stove into the tub. "All right, Johnny, you're first." Johnny and I and Verna all took turns. Later on in the evening Mama would pour clean water into the tub. Then she and Papa would retire to their bedroom so Miss Robbin could take her bath.

After we were sent upstairs to bed, I could hear Miss Robbin working at Mama's sewing machine, making my dress. Mama had the paddle of the butter churn going. She was keeping Miss Robbin company in the kitchen. If Miss Robbin and Mama got to be friends, I thought, maybe Mama wouldn't need me so much.

6

When Monday morning came, I had second thoughts about school. I nearly hid from Verna when it was time to go, but the crisp feel of my new dress and the ruffle around the skirt gave me courage. Mama had even found a yellow ribbon to make into a bow for my hair.

When we got near the schoolhouse, I started to get scared again, and Verna had to drag me along. A girl whose voice I didn't recognize came up to us. "Your sister's got a pretty dress, Verna," she said. Another girl named Effie said, "What did your sister do to her hair?" Just because I can't see, strangers think I can't hear either. Or they believe I am stupid. I was pleased, though, to hear the girls say I looked nice even if they didn't say it to me.

This time Miss Robbin let me sit with Verna instead of making me come up to the front of the classroom. And Carl kept quiet.

Miss Robbin said for our history lesson she was going to tell the class a story about the first president of the United States, George Washington. She wanted us all to listen carefully, and then she would ask us questions. If we knew the answers, we must raise our hands.

She told us lots of things. George Washington was born in 1732. He grew up in a four-room farmhouse on a river with a pretty name—the Rappahannock. He couldn't spell very well. He liked to wrestle and dance and act in plays. In the French and Indian War he had two horses shot from under him. Then she told us all about the Revolutionary War and how Washington didn't want to be president. When she finished, Miss Robbin started to ask us questions. I kept putting my hand up. I was used to listening hard and memorizing what I heard so I wouldn't lose it. Sometimes I was the only one who had the answer.

At recess Effie asked, "How did you know all those things?" Some girls took my hand and asked me to walk around the schoolyard with them. They said I had pretty hair and wanted to know if I minded not being able to see, and I told them, "Sure I do." Then they wanted to know if I just saw darkness, and I told them I didn't see anything. Pretty soon they stopped asking all those questions and started to talk about which boys they

liked best. Effie said she had a new baby sister that cried all night. Another girl said she
wished she lived in a big city, and someone
else said they hated to gather eggs because
the hens had fleas.

Verna started to take me back to class, and
the other girls ran on ahead. Halfway across
the playground I heard Carl Kleino's voice.
I stood still, holding tightly on to Verna's
hand. Carl said, "I didn't want to come up
to you when those dumb girls were there,
but I want to tell you I'm sorry about what
I said to you the other day." Then I heard
him hurrying away.

At the table that night I could hardly stop
talking about school. Finally, Mama told me
to eat my supper and let them have some
peace. Miss Robbin had been quiet all
through the meal. Just as we were finishing
dessert, she said, "I know what I'll do." I
heard her get up from the table, and then I

heard the kitchen door slam. In no time she was back and a lot of things rattled onto the table.

"What are you doing with those acorns?" Papa asked her.

"Well," she said, "I've been worrying about how I can teach Hannah arithmetic. Mr. Thomas, could you drill holes in these acorns for me? And Mrs. Thomas, could you loan me three knitting needles?"

Papa said to Miss Robbin, "You got some funny ideas." He went and drilled the holes anyhow. Mama got the knitting needles, and Johnny and Verna and I waited to find out what Miss Robbin was going to do.

"I'm sticking these needles through this heavy cardboard, Hannah, so they will stand up all by themselves. Then we'll make an abacus with the acorns. This is the way people counted two thousand years ago. This first needle will stand for ones, and the sec-

ond one for tens, and the third one for hundreds." She began to show me how I could add and subtract by adding and taking away acorns from the three needles.

"Well!" said Papa. "That's a clever trick if ever I saw one. It didn't cost a penny, either."

"There's one other thing, Mr. Thomas," Miss Robbin said. "There was a blind teacher, a Mr. Braille, who invented a way of printing books so that blind people could read. I know where I can get some books, but I wonder if we could send away for his device that lets blind people write?"

"Is it free?" Papa asked.

"No. I'm afraid it costs money."

"Well, you'll have to forget about that."

"Yes, sir," said Miss Robbin. But she didn't sound like she would forget. And I knew she hadn't, because one day she told all of us at school about Braille. She showed the class pictures of a contraption that made raised dots that let blind people read with their fingers and write by poking at the paper with something called a stylus. Verna described the pictures to me. Then she whispered, "Hannah, it says it costs five dollars!" I knew Papa would never be able to save that much, so I tried to forget about it.

7

The students at school were given three days off toward the end of October to help with the potato harvest. In the sandy soil of northern Michigan, potatoes were the best crop. Papa said all you had to do was tuck them into the ground in the spring and then stand back. Everyone, from the little children to the grandmothers and grandfathers, turned out for the harvest. People went from farm to farm to help their neighbors.

Each year there was a contest on the first day of the harvest. All the potato farmers chipped in some money, and whoever dug up the most potatoes got a prize. For the last two years Carl Kleino had won.

Afterwards there was a huge supper with singing and dancing. Next to Christmas, it was the biggest celebration of the year. Even though I couldn't help with the harvest, Mama and Papa always took me. This year Miss Robbin was going to dig potatoes too. "I've been teaching for three weeks. Now it's time I learned something," she said.

The harvest started at the Hermans' farm. The Hermans had the county's biggest potato fields. Mrs. Herman was a good cook, so everyone looked forward to the huge meal she put on. When the whistle blew to begin the contest, even Johnny ran out to dig potatoes. I was sitting by myself at the edge of the field where Mama and Papa had left me. I could hear the harvesters call to one another, making jokes about who was getting the most potatoes. Someone came up to me and said, "Come on, Hannah, you've got to help." It was Effie from school.

Verna was with her. "I'll show you where to dig, Hannah," Verna said. I let them lead me onto the potato field. "Carl is turning over the ground, so all we have to do is pick the potatoes up and put them in the bushel baskets," Effie said.

"Why is he letting us pick up his potatoes?" I asked. "He'll never win the contest that way."

"It was his idea," Verna said. By now I was reaching down into the soft, sandy ground for the potatoes. They had the earth's warmness. I found first one, and then another and another. Discovering gold, I thought, couldn't be more exciting.

I felt for the bushel basket next to me and dropped the potatoes in. When I heard other potatoes being dropped into the basket, I thought they were Effie's and Verna's. Someone kept coming up to leave a new basket and carry the full one away. I could hear the other students from school nearby.

I could hear Carl, too. He was urging everyone to work faster.

Hours went by. I moved down one furrow and up another, feeling for the hard lumps in the soft sand. My back ached and my shoes were filled with sand and my knees hurt from kneeling. I didn't care, though. I just wanted to get as many potatoes as I could. It felt wonderful to be doing what everyone else was doing.

Finally, just when I thought I couldn't heave another potato into a basket, the whistle blew. There were cries of "Hurrah!" I could hear giggles all around me. I recognized the voices from school. "Why is everyone laughing?" I asked Verna.

She was giggling too. "You'll find out," she said.

"Attention, everyone." It was Mr. Herman. "I have good news. This year we have a special prize of five dollars to award." At the mention of so large an amount, there was a lot of clapping and cheering. "All right. Quiet down. I know you are all waiting to hear who harvested the most potatoes. The winner is Hannah Thomas."

I couldn't believe my ears. I just stood where I was. "Go on up and get your prize, Hannah," called Papa. Miss Robbin gave me a hug, and Mama reached down and squeezed my hand.

Verna pulled me toward Mr. Herman. "How could I be the one to win?" I asked him.

"All I know," Mr. Herman said, "is that you filled the most baskets of potatoes. Here's the prize. Five dollars!" He counted five one-dollar bills into my hand.

All the children from school crowded around me, asking to see the dollar bills. "Verna, tell me what happened," I said.

"Carl turned over the dirt, and all of us

helped fill your basket. We wanted you to win the money. Now you can get that thing that makes dots and lets you write."

"Where's Carl?" I asked.

"He was here a minute ago," Effie said.

"He ran off," said Miss Robbin. I could tell from her voice she was smiling. "He's afraid he'll lose his reputation for being a bad boy."

Mrs. Herman called, "Time for supper." I suddenly felt hungry. I went running off with Verna and Effie toward the Hermans' house. All the while I was running I was thinking that this was the happiest day of my life and I would never forget it, because soon I would be able to write it down.

About the Author

"Near my home in northern Michigan is a one-room schoolhouse," says Gloria Whelan. "Old blackboards hang on the walls. Maps show the world as it was a hundred years ago. Across from the schoolhouse is the farm where the schoolteacher boarded.

"I began to think about what it was like to attend such a school. Then I imagined the farm family, the teacher, and a very special student whose life would be changed by meeting the teacher. And there were Hannah and Miss Robbin!"

Gloria Whelan is a poet and short-story writer. She has also written many books for children, including *Goodbye, Vietnam; Next Spring an Oriole;* and *Silver.*

About the Illustrator

Leslie Bowman was born in New York City, grew up in Connecticut, and graduated from the Rhode Island School of Design. "I like the nineteenth-century setting of *Hannah,*" she says, "and I had a lot of fun doing research to make sure I created the right historical atmosphere in the drawings." She has illustrated many children's books, including *Balloons and Other Poems, Snow Company,* and *The Canada Geese Quilt,* an ALA Notable Book. Leslie Bowman lives in Minnesota.